The Beatrix Potter
Collection
Volume One

THE BEATRIX POTTER COLLECTION

VOLUME ONE

WORDSWORTH CLASSICS

For my husband
ANTHONY JOHN RANSON
with love from your wife, the publisher.
Eternally grateful for your unconditional love.

Readers who are interested in other titles from
Wordsworth Editions are invited to visit our website at
www.wordsworth-editions.com

For our latest list and a full mail-order service, contact
Bibliophile Books, 5 Datapoint, South Crescent, London E16 4TL
TEL: +44 (0)20 7474 2474 FAX: +44 (0)20 7474 8589
ORDERS: orders@bibliophilebooks.com
WEBSITE: www.bibliophilebooks.com

First published in 2014 by Wordsworth Editions Limited
8B East Street, Ware, Hertfordshire SG12 9HJ

ISBN 978 1 84022 723 9

Wordsworth Editions
is the company founded in 1987 by
MICHAEL TRAYLER

Typeset in Great Britain by Antony Gray
Printed and bound by Clays Ltd, St Ives plc

The Beatrix Potter
Collection
Volume One

IN THIS BOOK

The Tale of Peter Rabbit

ONCE upon a time there were four little rabbits, and their names were — Flopsy, Mopsy, Cottontail and Peter.

They lived with their mother in a sandbank, underneath the root of a very big fir tree.

'Now, my dears,' said old Mrs Rabbit one morning, 'you may go into the fields or down the lane, but don't go into Mr McGregor's garden: your father had an accident there; he was put in a pie by Mrs McGregor.'

'Now run along, and don't get into mischief. I am going out.'

Then old Mrs Rabbit took a basket and her umbrella and went through the wood to the baker's. She bought a loaf of brown bread and five currant buns.

Flopsy, Mopsy and Cottontail, who were good little bunnies, went down the lane to gather blackberries.

But Peter, who was very naughty, ran straight away to Mr McGregor's garden, and squeezed under the gate!

First he ate some lettuces and some French beans; and then he ate some radishes.

And then, feeling rather sick, he went to look for some parsley.

But round the end of a cucumber frame, whom should he meet but Mr McGregor!

Mr McGregor was on his hands and knees planting out young cabbages, but he jumped up and ran after Peter, waving a rake and calling out, 'Stop thief.'

Peter was most dreadfully frightened; he rushed all over the garden, for he had forgotten the way back to the gate.

He lost one of his shoes among the cabbages, and the other shoe among the potatoes.

After losing them, he ran on four legs and went faster, so that I think he might have got away altogether if he had not unfortunately run into a gooseberry net and got caught by the large buttons on his jacket. It was a blue jacket with brass buttons, quite new.

The Tale of Peter Rabbit

Peter gave himself up for lost, and shed big tears; but his sobs were overheard by some friendly sparrows, who flew to him in great excitement and implored him to exert himself.

Mr McGregor came up with a sieve, which he intended to pop upon the top of Peter; but Peter wriggled out just in time, leaving his jacket behind him,

and rushed into the toolshed, and jumped into a can. It would have been a beautiful thing to hide in, if it had not had so much water in it.

Mr McGregor was quite sure that Peter was somewhere in the toolshed, perhaps hidden underneath a flower-pot. He began to turn them over carefully, looking under each.

Presently Peter sneezed – 'Kertyschoo!' Mr McGregor was after him in no time, and tried to put his foot upon Peter, who jumped out of a window, upsetting three plants. The window was too small for Mr McGregor and he was tired of running after Peter. He went back to his work.

Peter sat down to rest; he was out of breath and trembling with fright, and he had not the least idea which way to go. Also he was very damp with sitting in that can.

After a time he began to wander about, going lippity-lippity, not very fast, and

looking all around. He found a door in a wall; but it was locked, and there was no room for a fat little rabbit to squeeze underneath. An old mouse was running in and out over the stone doorstep, carrying peas and beans to her family in the wood. Peter asked her the way to the gate, but she had such a large pea in her mouth that she could not answer. She only shook her head at him.

Peter began to cry.

Then he tried to find his way straight across the garden, but he became more and more puzzled. Presently, he came to a pond where Mr McGregor filled his water-cans. A white cat was staring at

some goldfish; she sat very, very still, but now and then the tip of her tail twitched as if it were alive.

Peter thought it best to go away without speaking to her; he had heard about cats from his cousin, little Benjamin Bunny.

He went back towards the toolshed, but suddenly, quite close to him, he heard the noise of a hoe — scr-r-ritch, scratch, scratch, scritch. Peter scuttered underneath the bushes. But presently, as nothing happened, he came out, and climbed upon a wheelbarrow, and peeped over. The first thing he saw was Mr McGregor hoeing onions. His back was turned towards Peter and beyond him was the gate!

Peter got down very quietly off the wheelbarrow, and started running as fast as he could go, along a straight walk behind some blackcurrant bushes.

Mr McGregor caught sight of him at the corner, but Peter did not care. He slipped underneath the gate and was safe at last in the wood outside the garden.

Mr McGregor hung up the little jacket and the shoes for a scarecrow to frighten the blackbirds.

Peter never stopped running or looked behind him till he got home to the big fir tree.

He was so tired that he flopped down upon the nice soft sand on the floor of the rabbit-hole and shut his eyes. His mother was busy cooking; she wondered what he had done with his clothes. It was the second little jacket and pair of shoes that Peter had lost in a fortnight!

I am sorry to say that Peter was not very well during the evening.

His mother put him to bed, and made some camomile tea; and she gave a dose of it to Peter!

'One tablespoonful to be taken at bedtime.'

But Flopsy, Mopsy and Cottontail had bread and milk and blackberries for supper.

The Tale of
Squirrel Nutkin

A story for
Norah

This is a tale about a tail — a tail that belonged to a little red squirrel, and his name was Nutkin.

He had a brother called Twinkleberry, and a great many cousins; they lived in a wood at the edge of a lake.

In the middle of the lake there was an island covered with trees and nut bushes; and among those trees stood a hollow oak tree, which was the house of an owl who was called Old Brown.

The Tale of Squirrel Nutkin

One autumn when the nuts were ripe, and the leaves on the hazel bushes were golden and green, Nutkin and Twinkleberry and all the other little squirrels came out of the wood and down to the edge of the lake.

They made little rafts out of twigs, and they paddled away over the water to Owl Island to gather nuts.

Each squirrel had a little sack and a large oar, and spread out his tail for a sail.

They also took with them an offering of three fat mice as a present for Old Brown, and put them down upon his doorstep.

Then Twinkleberry and the other little squirrels each made a low bow, and said politely, 'Old Mr Brown, will you favour us with permission to gather nuts upon your island?'

But Nutkin was excessively impertinent in his manners. He bobbed up and down like a little red *cherry*, singing:

'Riddle-me, riddle-me, rot-tot-tote!
A little wee man, in a red, red coat!
A staff in his hand, and a stone in his throat;
If you'll tell me this riddle, I'll give you a groat.'

Now this riddle is as old as the hills; Mr Brown paid no attention whatever to Nutkin.

He shut his eyes obstinately and went to sleep.

The Tale of Squirrel Nutkin

The squirrels filled their little sacks with nuts, and sailed away home in the evening.

But next morning they all came back again to Owl Island; and Twinkleberry and the others brought a fine fat mole, and laid it on the stone in front of Old Brown's doorway, and said, 'Mr Brown, will you favour us with your gracious permission to gather some more nuts?'

But Nutkin, who had no respect, began to dance up and down, tickling old Mr Brown with a *nettle* and singing:

> *'Old Mr B! Riddle-me-ree!*
> *Hitty Pitty within the wall,*
> *Hitty Pitty without the wall;*
> *If you touch Hitty Pitty,*
> *Hitty Pitty will bite you!'*

Mr Brown woke up suddenly and carried the mole into his house.

The Tale of Squirrel Nutkin

He shut the door in Nutkin's face. Presently a little thread of blue *smoke* from a wood fire came up from the top of the tree, and Nutkin peeped through the keyhole and sang:

'A house full, a hole full!
And you cannot gather a bowl-full!'

The Tale of Squirrel Nutkin

The squirrels searched for nuts all over the island and filled their little sacks.

But Nutkin gathered oak-apples — yellow and scarlet — and sat upon a beech-stump playing marbles, and watching the door of old Mr Brown.

On the third day the squirrels got up very early and went fishing; they caught seven fat minnows as a present for Old Brown.

They paddled over the lake and landed under a crooked chestnut tree on Owl Island.

Twinkleberry and six other little squirrels each carried a fat minnow; but Nutkin, who had no nice manners, brought no present at all. He ran in front, singing:

'The man in the wilderness said to me,
"How may strawberries grow in the sea?"
I answered him as I thought good —
"As many red herrings as grow in the wood." '

But old Mr Brown took no interest in riddles — not even when the answer was provided for him.

On the fourth day the squirrels brought a present of six fat beetles, which were as good as plums in *plum-pudding* for Old Brown. Each beetle was wrapped up carefully in a dock leaf fastened with a pine-needle pin.

But Nutkin sang as rudely as ever:

The Tale of Squirrel Nutkin

'Old Mr B! riddle-me-ree!

Flour of England, fruit of Spain,

Met together in a shower of rain;

Put in a bag tied round with a string,

If you'll tell me this riddle,

I'll give you a ring!'

Which was ridiculous of Nutkin, because he had not got any ring to give to Old Brown.

The other squirrels hunted up and down the nut bushes; but Nutkin gathered robin's pincushions off a briar bush, and stuck them full of pine-needle pins.

On the fifth day the squirrels brought a present of wild honey; it was so sweet and sticky that they licked their fingers as they put it down upon the stone. They had stolen it out of a bumble *bees'* nest on the tippity top of the hill.

But Nutkin skipped up and down, singing:

'Hum-a-bum! buzz! buzz! Hum-a-bum buzz!
As I went over Tippletine
I met a flock of bonny swine;
Some yellow-nacked, some yellow backed!
They were the very bonniest swine
That e'er went over Tippletine.'

Old Mr Brown turned up his eyes in disgust at the impertinence of Nutkin.

But he ate up the honey!

The Tale of Squirrel Nutkin

The squirrels filled their little sacks with nuts.

But Nutkin climbed upon a big flat rock and played ninepins with a crab apple and green fir-cones.

On the sixth day, which was Saturday, the squirrels came again for the last time; they brought a new-laid *egg* in a little rush basket as a parting present for Old Brown.

But Nutkin ran in front laughing, and shouting:

> *'Humpty Dumpty lies in the beck,*
> *With a white counterpane round his neck;*
> *Forty doctors and forty wrights,*
> *Cannot put Humpty Dumpty to rights!'*

Now old Mr Brown took an interest in eggs; he opened one eye and shut it again. But still he did not speak.

Nutkin became more and more impertinent:

> *'Old Mr B! Old Mr B!*
> *Hickamore Hackamore on the*
>   *king's kitchen door;*
> *All the king's horses, and all the king's men,*

The Tale of Squirrel Nutkin

Couldn't drive Hickamore Hackamore
Off the king's kitchen door!'

Nutkin danced up and down like a *sunbeam*; but still Old Brown said nothing at all.

Nutkin began again:

'Authur O'Bower has broken his band,
He comes roaring up the land!
The King of Scots with all his power,
Cannot turn Arthur of the Bower!'

Nutkin made a whirring noise to sound like the *wind* and he took a

running jump right on to the head of
Old Brown! . . .

Then all at once there was a flutterment
and a scufflement and a loud, 'Squeak!'

The other squirrels scuttered away
into the bushes.

When they came back very cautiously, peeping round the tree, there was Old Brown sitting on his doorstep, quite still, with his eyes closed, as if nothing had happened.

✳   ✳   ✳

The Tale of Squirrel Nutkin

But Nutkin was in his waistcoat pocket!
This looks like the end of the story;
but it isn't.

Old Brown carried Nutkin into his house, and held him up by the tail, intending to skin him; but Nutkin pulled so very hard that his tail broke in two, and he dashed up the staircase and escaped out of the attic window.

The Tale of Squirrel Nutkin

And to this day, if you meet Nutkin up a tree and ask him a riddle, he will throw sticks at you, and stamp his feet and scold, and shout –

'Cuck-cuck-cuck-cur-r-r-cuck-k!'

The Tailor of Gloucester

> *'I'll be at charges for a looking-glass;*
> *And entertain a score or two of tailors.'*

William Shakespeare, RICHARD III

My dear Freda — Because you are fond of fairytales, and have been ill, I have made you a story all for yourself — a new one that nobody has read before.

And the queerest thing about it is that I heard it in Gloucestershire, and that it is true — at least about the tailor, the waistcoat, and the 'No more twist'!

Christmas 1901

In the time of swords and periwigs and full-skirted coats with flowered lappets – when gentlemen wore ruffles and gold-laced waistcoats of paduasoy and taffeta – there lived a tailor in Gloucester.

He sat in the window of a little shop in Westgate Street, cross-legged on a table, from morning till dark.

All day long while the light lasted he sewed and snippeted, piecing out his satin and pompadour and lutestring; stuffs had strange names, and were very expensive in the days of the Tailor of Gloucester.

But although he sewed fine silk for his neighbours, he himself was very, very poor – a little old man in spectacles, with a pinched face, old crooked fingers and a suit of threadbare clothes.

He cut his coats without waste, according to his embroidered cloth; they were very small ends and snippets that lay about upon the table – 'Too narrow breadths for nought – except waistcoats for mice,' said the tailor.

One bitter cold day near Christmastime the tailor began to make a coat – a coat of cherry-coloured corded silk embroidered with pansies and roses – and a cream-coloured satin waistcoat, trimmed with gauze and green worsted chenille, for the Mayor of Gloucester.

The tailor worked and worked, and he talked to himself. He measured the silk, and turned it round and round, and

The Tailor of Gloucester

trimmed it into shape with his shears; the table was all littered with cherry-coloured snippets.

'No breadth at all, and cut on the cross; it is no breadth at all; tippets for mice and ribbons for mobs! for mice!' said the Tailor of Gloucester.

When the snowflakes came down

against the small leaded windowpanes and shut out the light, the tailor had done his day's work; all the silk and satin lay cut out upon the table.

There were twelve pieces for the coat and four pieces for the waistcoat; and there were pocket flaps and cuffs, and buttons all in order. For the lining of the coat there was fine yellow taffeta, and for the buttonholes of the waistcoat there was cherry-coloured twist. And everything was ready to sew together in the morning, all measured and sufficient — except that there was wanting just one single skein of cherry-coloured twisted silk.

The tailor came out of his shop at dark, for he did not sleep there at nights; he fastened the window and locked the door and took away the key. No one lived there at night but little brown mice, and they run in and out without any keys!

The Tailor of Gloucester

For behind the wooden wainscots of all the old houses in Gloucester, there are little mouse staircases and secret trapdoors; and the mice run from house to house through those long narrow passages; they can run all over the town without going into the streets.

But the tailor came out of his shop and shuffled home through the snow. He lived quite near by in College Court, next the doorway to College Green; and although it was not a big house, the tailor was so poor he only rented the kitchen.

He lived alone with his cat; he was called Simpkin.

Now all day long while the tailor was out at work, Simpkin kept house by

himself; and he also was fond of the mice, though he gave them no satin for coats!

'Miaow?' said the cat when the tailor opened the door. 'Miaow?'

The tailor replied – 'Simpkin, we shall make our fortune, but I am worn to a ravelling. Take this groat (which is our last fourpence) and, Simpkin, take a china pipkin; buy a penn'orth of bread, a penn'orth of milk and a penn'orth of sausages. And oh, Simpkin, with the last penny of our fourpence buy me one penn'orth of cherry-coloured silk. But do not lose the last penny of the fourpence, Simpkin, or I am undone and worn to a thread-paper, for I have *no more twist.*'

Then Simpkin again said, 'Miaow?' and took the groat and the pipkin and went out into the dark.

The tailor was very tired and

beginning to be ill. He sat down by the
hearth and talked to himself about that
wonderful coat.

'I shall make my fortune — to be cut bias — the Mayor of Gloucester is to be married on Christmas Day in the morning, and he has ordered a coat and an embroidered waistcoat — to be lined with yellow taffeta — and the taffeta suffices; there is no more left over in snippets than will serve to make tippets for mice — '

Then the tailor started; for suddenly, interrupting him, from the dresser at the other side of the kitchen came a number of little noises — *Tip tap, tip tap. Tip tap tip!*

'Now what can that be?' said the Tailor of Gloucester, jumping up from his chair. The dresser was covered with crockery and pipkins, willow-pattern plates and teacups and mugs.

The tailor crossed the kitchen and stood quite still beside the dresser, listening and peering through his spectacles. Again from under a teacup

came those funny little noises – *Tip tap, tip tap. Tip tap tip!*

'This is very peculiar,' said the Tailor of Gloucester; and he lifted up the teacup which was upside down.

Out stepped a little live lady mouse, and made a curtsey to the tailor! Then she hopped away down off the dresser and under the wainscot.

The tailor sat down again by the fire, warming his poor cold hands, and mumbling to himself: 'The waistcoat is cut out from peach-coloured satin — tambour stitch and rosebuds in beautiful floss silk. Was I wise to entrust my last fourpence to Simpkin? One-and-twenty buttonholes of cherry-coloured twist!'

But all at once, from the dresser, there came other little noises: *Tip tap, tip tap, tip tap tip!*

'This is passing extraordinary!' said the Tailor of Gloucester, and turned over another teacup, which was upside down.

Out stepped a little gentleman mouse, and made a bow to the tailor!

And then from all over the dresser came a chorus of little tappings, all

sounding together, and answering one another, like watch-beetles in an old worm-eaten window-shutter — *Tip tap, tip tap, tip tap tip!*

And out from under teacups and from under bowls and basins stepped other and more little mice who hopped away down off the dresser and under the wainscot.

The tailor sat down, close over the fire, lamenting – 'One-and-twenty button-holes of cherry-coloured silk! To be finished by noon of Saturday, and this is Tuesday evening. Was it right to let loose those mice, undoubtedly the property of Simpkin? Alack, I am undone, for I have no more twist!'

The little mice came out again, and listened to the tailor; they took notice of the pattern of that wonderful coat. They whispered to one another about the taffeta lining, and about little mouse tippets.

And then all at once they all ran away together down the passage behind the wainscot, squeaking and calling to one another as they ran from house to house; and not one mouse was left in the tailor's kitchen when Simpkin came back with the pipkin of milk!

Simpkin opened the door and bounced

in, with an angry 'G-r-r-Miaow!' like a cat that is vexed: for he hated the snow, and there was snow in his ears, and snow in his collar at the back of his neck. He put down the loaf and the sausages upon the dresser and sniffed.

'Simpkin,' said the tailor, 'where is my twist?'

But Simpkin set down the pipkin of milk upon the dresser, and looked suspiciously at the teacups. He wanted his supper of little fat mouse!

'Simpkin,' said the tailor, 'where is my *twist?*'

But Simpkin hid a little parcel privately in the teapot, and spat and growled at the tailor; and if Simpkin had been able to talk, he would have asked: 'Where is my *mouse?*'

'Alack, I am undone!' said the Tailor of Gloucester, and went sadly to bed.

All that night long Simpkin hunted and searched through the kitchen, peeping into cupboards and under the

wainscot, and into the teapot where he
had hidden that twist; but still he found
never a mouse!

Whenever the tailor muttered and

talked in his sleep, Simpkin said, 'Miaow-ger-r-w-s-s-ch!' and made strange horrid noises, as cats do at night.

For the poor old tailor was very ill with a fever, tossing and turning in his four-post bed; and still in his dreams he mumbled — 'No more twist! No more twist!'

All that day he was ill, and the next day, and the next; and what should become of the cherry-coloured coat? In the tailor's shop in Westgate Street the embroidered silk and satin lay cut out upon the table — one-and-twenty button-holes — and who should come to sew them, when the window was barred, and the door was fast locked?

But that does not hinder the little

brown mice; they run in and out without any keys through all the old houses in Gloucester!

Out of doors the market folks went trudging through the snow to buy their geese and turkeys and to bake their Christmas pies; but there would be no Christmas dinner for Simpkin and the poor old Tailor of Gloucester.

The tailor lay ill for three days and nights; and then it was Christmas Eve, and very late at night. The moon climbed up over the roofs and chimneys, and looked down over the gateway into College Court. There were no lights in the windows, nor any sound in the houses; all the city of Gloucester was fast asleep under the snow.

And still Simpkin wanted his mice, and he mewed as he stood beside the four-post bed.

But it is in the old story that all the

beasts can talk on the night between Christmas Eve and Christmas Day in the morning (though there are very few folk that can hear them, or know what it is that they say).

When the Cathedral clock struck twelve there was an answer — like an echo of the chimes — and Simpkin heard it, and came out of the tailor's door, and wandered about in the snow.

From all the roofs and gables and old wooden houses in Gloucester came a thousand merry voices singing the old Christmas rhymes — all the old songs that ever I heard of, and some that I don't know, like Whittington's bells

First and loudest the cocks cried out: 'Dame, get up, and bake your pies!'

'Oh, dilly, dilly, dilly!' sighed Simpkin. And now in a garret there were lights and sounds of dancing, and cats came from over the way.

'Hey, diddle, diddle, the cat and the fiddle! All the cats in Gloucester — except me,' said Simpkin.

Under the wooden eaves the starlings

and sparrows sang of Christmas pies; the jackdaws woke up in the Cathedral tower; and although it was the middle of the night the throstles and robins sang; the air was quite full of little twittering tunes. But it was all rather provoking to poor hungry Simpkin!

Particularly he was vexed with some little shrill voices from behind a wooden lattice. I think that they were bats, because they always have very small voices — especially in a black frost, when they talk in their sleep, like the Tailor of Gloucester.

They said something mysterious that sounded like:

'"Buz," quoth the blue fly, "Hum," quoth the bee; "Buz" and "Hum" they cry, and so do we!'

and Simpkin went away shaking his ears as if he had a bee in his bonnet.

From the tailor's shop in Westgate came a glow of light; and when Simpkin crept up to peep in at the window it was full of candles. There was a snippeting of scissors, and snappeting of thread; and little mouse voices sang loudly and gaily:

> *'Four-and-twenty tailors*
> *Went to catch a snail,*
> *The best man among them*
> *Durst not touch her tail;*
> *She put out her horns*
> *Like a little kyloe cow,*
> *"Run, tailors, run! or she'll have you all e'en now!"'*

Then without a pause the little mouse voices went on again:

'Sieve my lady's oatmeal,
Grind my lady's flour,
Put it in a chestnut,
Let it stand an hour —'

'Mew! Mew!' interrupted Simpkin, and he scratched at the door. But, as the key was under the tailor's pillow, he could not get in.

The little mice only laughed, and tried another tune:

'Three little mice sat down to spin,
 Pussy passed by and she peeped in.
"What are you at, my fine little men?"
"Making coats for gentlemen."
"Shall I come in and cut off your threads?"
"Oh, no, Miss Pussy, you'd bite off our heads!"'

'Mew! Mew!' cried Simpkin.

'Hey diddle dinketty!' answered the little mice:

'Hey diddle dinketty, poppetty pet!
The merchants of London they wear scarlet;
Silk in the collar, and gold in the hem,
So merrily march the merchantmen!'

They clicked their thimbles to mark

the time, but none of the songs pleased
Simpkin; he sniffed and mewed at the
door of the shop.

> 'And then I bought
> A pipkin and a popkin,
> A slipkin and a slopkin,
> All for one farthing —

and upon the kitchen dresser!' added the rude little mice.

'Mew! scratch! scratch!' scuffled Simpkin on the window-sill; while the little mice inside sprang to their feet, and all began to shout at once in little twittering voices: 'No more twist! No more twist!'

And they barred up the window shutters and shut out Simpkin.

But still through the nicks in the shutters he could hear the click of thimbles, and little mouse voices singing:

'No more twist! No more twist!'

Simpkin came away from the shop and went home, considering in his mind. He found the poor old tailor without fever, sleeping peacefully.

Then Simpkin went on tiptoe and took the little parcel of silk out of the teapot, and looked at it in the moonlight; and he felt quite ashamed of his badness compared with those good little mice!

When the tailor awoke in the morning, the first thing he saw upon the patchwork quilt was a skein of

cherry-coloured twisted silk, and beside
his bed stood the repentant Simpkin!

'Alack, I am worn to a ravelling,' said
the Tailor of Gloucester, 'but I have my
twist!'

The sun was shining on the snow when the tailor got up and dressed, and came out into the street with Simpkin running before him.

The starlings whistled on the chimney stacks, and the throstles and robins sang –

but they sang their own little noises, not the words they had sung in the night.

'Alack,' said the tailor, 'I have my twist; but no more strength — nor time — than will serve to make me one single button-hole; for this is Christmas Day in the morning! The Mayor of Gloucester shall be married by noon — and where is his cherry-coloured coat?'

He unlocked the door of the little shop in Westgate Street, and Simpkin ran in, like a cat that expects something.

But there was no one there! Not even one little brown mouse!

The boards were swept clean; the little ends of thread and the little silk snippets were all tidied away, and gone from off the floor.

But upon the table – oh joy! the tailor gave a shout – there, where he had left plain cuttings of silk – there lay the most beautifullest coat and embroidered satin waistcoat that ever were worn by a Mayor of Gloucester.

There were roses and pansies upon the facings of the coat; and the waistcoat was worked with poppies and cornflowers.

Everything was finished except just one single cherry-coloured buttonhole, and where that buttonhole was wanting there was pinned a scrap of paper with these words – in little teeny-weeny writing: *No more twist.*

And from then began the luck of the Tailor of Gloucester; he grew quite stout, and he grew quite rich.

He made the most wonderful waist-coats for all the rich merchants of Gloucester, and for all the fine gentlemen of the country round.

Never were seen such ruffles, or such embroidered cuffs and lappets! But his

buttonholes were the greatest triumph of all.

The stitches of those buttonholes were so neat — *so* neat — I wonder how they could be stitched by an old man in

spectacles, with crooked old fingers, and a tailor's thimble.

The stitches of those buttonholes were *so* small — *so* small — they looked as if they had been made by little mice!

The Tale of Benjamin Bunny

To the Children of Sawrey
from Old Mr Bunny

One morning a little rabbit sat on a bank. He pricked his ears and listened to the trit-trot, trit-trot of a pony.

A gig was coming along the road; it was driven by Mr McGregor, and beside him sat Mrs McGregor in her best bonnet.

As soon as they had passed, little Benjamin Bunny slid down into the road, and set off – with a hop, skip and a jump – to call upon his relations, who lived in the wood at the back of Mr McGregor's garden.

The Tale of Benjamin Bunny

That wood was full of rabbit holes; and in the neatest, sandiest hole of all lived Benjamin's aunt and his cousins – Flopsy, Mopsy, Cottontail and Peter.

Old Mrs Rabbit was a widow; she earned her living by knitting rabbit-wool mittens and muffatees (I once bought a pair at a bazaar). She also sold herbs, and rosemary tea, and rabbit-tobacco (which is what *we* call lavender).

Little Benjamin did not very much want to see his aunt.

He came round the back of the fir tree

and nearly tumbled upon the top of his cousin Peter.

Peter was sitting by himself. He looked poorly, and was dressed in a red cotton pocket-handkerchief.

'Peter,' said little Benjamin, in a whisper, 'who has got your clothes?'

Peter replied, 'The scarecrow in Mr McGregor's garden,' and described how he had been chased about the garden, and had dropped his shoes and coat.

Little Benjamin sat down beside his cousin and assured him that Mr McGregor had gone out in a gig, and Mrs McGregor also; and certainly for the day, because she was wearing her best bonnet.

Peter said he hoped that it would rain.

At this point old Mrs Rabbit's voice was heard inside the rabbit hole calling: 'Cottontail! Cottontail! fetch some more camomile!'

Peter said he thought he might feel better if he went for a walk.

They went away hand in hand, and got upon the flat top of the wall at the bottom of the wood. From here they looked down into Mr McGregor's garden. Peter's coat and shoes were plainly to be seen upon the scarecrow,

topped with an old tam-o'-shanter of Mr McGregor's.

Little Benjamin said: 'It spoils people's clothes to squeeze under a gate; the proper way to get in is to climb down a pear tree.'

Peter fell down head first; but it was of no consequence as the bed below was newly raked and quite soft.

It had been sown with lettuces.

They left a great many odd little footmarks all over the bed, especially little Benjamin, who was wearing clogs.

Little Benjamin said that the first thing to be done was to get back

Peter's clothes, in order that they might be able to use the pocket-handkerchief.

They took them off the scarecrow. There had been rain during the night so there was water in the shoes, and the coat was somewhat shrunk.

Benjamin tried on the tam-o'-shanter, but it was too big for him.

Then he suggested that they should fill the pocket-handkerchief with onions, as a little present for his aunt.

Peter did not seem to be enjoying himself; he kept hearing noises.

Benjamin, on the contrary, was perfectly at home, and ate a lettuce leaf.

He said that he was in the habit of coming to the garden with his father to get lettuces for their Sunday dinner.

(The name of little Benjamin's papa was old Mr Benjamin Bunny.)

The lettuces certainly were very fine.

Peter did not eat anything; he said he should like to go home. Presently he dropped half the onions.

Little Benjamin said that it was not possible to get back up the pear tree with a load of vegetables. He led the way

boldly towards the other end of the garden. They went along a little walk on planks, under a sunny red-brick wall.

The mice sat on their doorsteps cracking cherry-stones; they winked

at Peter Rabbit and little Benjamin
Bunny.

Presently Peter let the pocket-handkerchief go again.

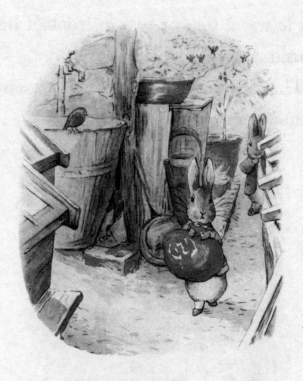

They got among flowerpots and frames and tubs. Peter heard noises worse than ever; his eyes were as big as lollypops!

He was a step or two in front of his cousin when he suddenly stopped.

This is what those little rabbits saw round that corner!

The Tale of Benjamin Bunny

Little Benjamin took one look, and then, in half a minute less than no time, he hid himself and Peter and the onions underneath a large basket . . .

The cat got up and stretched herself, then came and sniffed at the basket.

Perhaps she liked the smell of onions!

Anyway, she sat down upon the top of the basket.

She sat there for *five hours*.

I cannot draw you a picture of Peter and Benjamin underneath the basket, because it was quite dark, and because the smell of onions was fearful; it made Peter Rabbit and little Benjamin cry.

The sun got round behind the wood,

The Tale of Benjamin Bunny

and it was quite late in the afternoon; but still the cat sat upon the basket.

At length there was a pitter-patter, pitter-patter, and some bits of mortar fell from the wall above. The cat looked up and saw old Mr Benjamin Bunny prancing along the top of the wall

of the upper terrace. He was smoking a pipe of rabbit-tobacco, and had a little switch in his hand.

He was looking for his son.

Old Mr Bunny had no opinion whatever of cats. He took a tremendous jump off the top of the wall on to the top of the cat, and cuffed her off the basket, and kicked her into the greenhouse, scratching off a handful of fur.

The cat was too much surprised to scratch back.

When old Mr Bunny had driven the cat into the greenhouse, he locked the door.

Then he came back to the basket and took out his son Benjamin by the ears and whipped him with the little switch.

Then he took out his nephew Peter.

Then he took out the handkerchief of onions and marched out of the garden.

When Mr McGregor returned about half an hour later he observed several things which perplexed him.

It looked as though some person had been walking all over the garden in a pair of clogs – only the footmarks were too ridiculously little!

Also he could not understand how the cat could have managed to shut herself up *inside* the greenhouse, locking the door upon the *outside*.

When Peter got home his mother forgave him, because she was so glad to see that he had found his shoes and coat. Cottontail and Peter folded up the pocket-handkerchief and old Mrs Rabbit strung up the onions and hung them from the kitchen ceiling, with the bunches of herbs and the rabbit-tobacco.

The Tale of Two Bad Mice

For W. M. L. W.,
the little girl who had
the doll's house.

Once upon a time there was a very beautiful doll's-house; it was red brick with white windows, and it had real muslin curtains and a front door and a chimney.

It belonged to two dolls called Lucinda and Jane; at least it belonged to Lucinda, but she never ordered meals.

Jane was the cook; but she never did

any cooking, because the dinner had been bought ready-made, in a box full of shavings.

There were two red lobsters and a ham, a fish, a pudding and some pears and oranges.

They would not come off the plates, but they were extremely beautiful.

One morning Lucinda and Jane had gone out for a drive in the doll's perambulator. There was no one in the nursery, and it was very quiet. Presently there was a little scuffling, scratching

The Tale of Two Bad Mice

noise in a corner near the fireplace, where there was a hole under the skirting-board.

Tom Thumb put out his head for a moment, and then popped it in again. Tom Thumb was a mouse.

A minute afterwards, Hunca Munca, his wife, put her head out, too; and when she saw that there was no one in the nursery, she ventured out on the oilcloth under the coal-box.

The doll's-house stood at the other side of the fireplace. Tom Thumb and Hunca Munca went cautiously across the hearthrug. They pushed the front door — it was not fast.

Tom Thumb and Hunca Munca went upstairs and peeped into the dining-room. Then they squeaked with joy!

Such a lovely dinner was laid out upon the table! There were tin spoons, and lead knives and forks, and two dolly-chairs — all *so* convenient!

Tom Thumb set to work at once to carve the ham. It was a beautiful shiny yellow, streaked with red.

The knife crumpled up and hurt him; he put his finger in his mouth.

'It is not boiled enough; it is hard. You have a try, Hunca Munca.'

Hunca Munca stood up in her chair, and chopped at the ham with another lead knife.

'It's as hard as the hams at the cheesemonger's,' said Hunca Munca.

The ham broke off the plate with a jerk, and rolled under the table.

'Let it alone,' said Tom Thumb; 'give me some fish, Hunca Munca!'

Hunca Munca tried every tin spoon in turn; the fish was glued to the dish.

Then Tom Thumb lost his temper. He put the ham in the middle of the floor, and hit it with the tongs and with the shovel — bang, bang, smash, smash!

The ham flew all into pieces, for underneath the shiny paint it was made of nothing but plaster!

Then there was no end to the rage and disappointment of Tom Thumb and Hunca Munca. They broke up the pudding, the lobsters, the pears and the oranges.

As the fish would not come off the plate, they put it into the red-hot crinkly-paper fire in the kitchen; but it would

not burn either. Tom Thumb went up the kitchen chimney and looked out at the top — there was no soot.

While Tom Thumb was up the chimney, Hunca Munca had another disappointment. She found some tiny canisters upon the dresser, labelled Rice, Coffee and Sago, but when she turned them upside down, there was nothing inside except red and blue beads.

Then those mice set to work to do all the mischief they could – especially Tom Thumb! He took Jane's clothes out of the chest of drawers in her bedroom, and he threw them out of the top-floor window.

But Hunca Munca had a frugal mind. After pulling half the feathers out of Lucinda's bolster, she remembered that she herself was in want of a feather bed.

With Tom Thumbs's assistance she
carried the bolster downstairs, and across
the hearth rug. It was difficult to squeeze
the bolster into the mouse-hole; but they
managed it somehow.

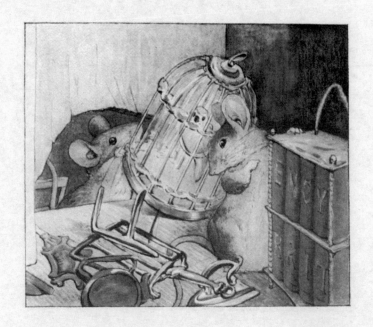

Then Hunca Munca went back and fetched a chair, a bookcase, a bird-cage, and several small odds and ends. The bookcase and the bird-cage refused to go into the mouse-hole.

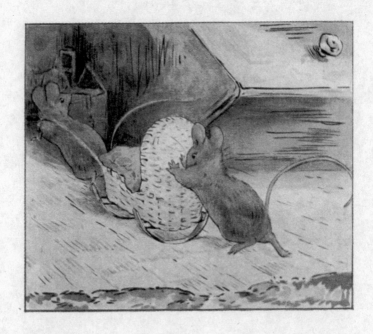

Hunca Munca left them behind the coal-box and went to fetch a cradle.

Hunca Munca was just returning with another chair, when suddenly there was a noise of talking outside upon the landing.

The mice rushed back to their hole,
and the dolls came into the nursery.

What a sight met the eyes of Jane and Lucinda! Lucinda sat upon the upset kitchen stove and stared; and Jane leant

against the kitchen dresser and smiled —
but neither of them made any remark.
The bookcase and the birdcage were
rescued from under the coal-box — but
Hunca Munca has got the cradle, and
some of Lucinda's clothes.

She also has some useful pots and pans, and several other things.

The little girl that the doll's-house belonged to, said, 'I will get a doll dressed like a policeman!'

But the nurse said, 'I will set a mousetrap!'

So that is the story of the Two Bad Mice — but they were not so very, very naughty after all, because Tom Thumb paid for everything he broke.

He found a crooked sixpence under the hearth rug; and upon Christmas Eve, he and Hunca Munca stuffed it into one of the stockings of Lucinda and Jane.

And very early every morning – before anybody is awake – Hunca Munca comes with her dustpan and her broom to sweep the dollies' house!

The Tale of
the Pie and
the Patty-Pan

Pussy-cat sits by the fire — how should she be fair?
In walks the little dog — says, 'Pussy are you there?
How do you do, Mistress Pussy? Mistress Pussy,
                                        how do you do?'
'I thank you kindly, little dog, I fare as well as you!'

OLD RHYME

For
Joan
to read to baby

Once upon a time there was a pussy-cat called Ribby who invited a little dog called Duchess to tea.

'Come in good time, my dear Duchess,' said Ribby's letter, 'and we will have something so very nice. I am baking it in a pie-dish — a pink-and-white pie-dish. You will never have tasted anything so good! And *you* shall eat it *all*! I will eat muffins, my dear Duchess!' wrote Ribby.

Duchess read the letter and wrote an answer: 'I will come with much pleasure at a quarter past four. But it is very strange. *I* was just going to invite you to come here to supper, my dear Ribby, to eat something *most delicious.*

'I will come very punctually, my dear Ribby,' wrote Duchess; and then at the end she added – 'I hope it isn't mouse?'

And then she thought that did not look quite polite; so she scratched out 'isn't mouse' and changed it to 'I hope it will be fine', and she gave her letter to the postman.

But she thought a great deal about Ribby's pie, and she read Ribby's letter over and over again.

'I am dreadfully afraid it *will* be mouse!' said Duchess to herself – 'I really couldn't, *couldn't* eat mouse pie.

The Pie and the Patty-Pan

And I shall have to eat it because it is a party. And *my* pie was going to be veal and ham. A pink-and-white pie-dish? and so is mine! just like Ribby's dish; they were both bought at Tabitha Twitchit's.'

Duchess went into her larder and took the pie off a shelf and looked at it.

'It is all ready to put into the oven.

Such lovely pie-crust; and I put in a little tin patty-pan to hold up the crust; and I made a hole in the middle with a fork to let out the steam – Oh, I do wish I could eat my own pie, instead of a pie made of mouse!'

Duchess considered and considered and read Ribby's letter again: 'A pink-and-white pie-dish – and *you* shall eat it *all.* "You" means me – then Ribby is not even going to taste the pie herself? A pink-and-white pie-dish! Ribby is sure to go out to buy the muffins . . . Oh, what a good idea! Why shouldn't I rush along and put my pie into Ribby's oven when Ribby isn't there?'

Duchess was quite delighted with her own cleverness!

Ribby in the meantime had received Duchess's answer, and as soon as she was sure that the little dog could come – she popped *her* pie into the oven. There were two ovens, one above the other; some other knobs and handles were only ornamental and not intended to open. Ribby put the pie into the lower oven; the door was very stiff.

'The top oven bakes too quickly,' said

Ribby to herself. 'It is a pie of the most
delicate and tender mouse minced up

with bacon. And I have taken out all the bones because Duchess did nearly choke herself with a fishbone last time I gave a party. She eats a little fast – rather big mouthfuls. But a most genteel and elegant little dog; infinitely superior company to Cousin Tabitha Twitchit.'

Ribby put on some coal and swept up the hearth. Then she went out with a can to the well for water to fill up the kettle.

Then she began to set the room in order, for it was the sitting-room as well as the kitchen. She shook the mats out at the front-door and put them straight; the hearth rug was a rabbit-skin. She dusted the clock and the ornaments on the mantelpiece, and she polished and rubbed the tables and chairs.

Then she spread a very clean white tablecloth, and set out her best china tea-set, which she took out of a wall-cupboard near the fireplace. The tea-cups were white with a pattern of pink roses; and the dinner-plates were white and blue.

When Ribby had laid the table she took a jug and a blue-and-white dish, and went out down the field to the farm, to fetch milk and butter.

When she came back, she peeped into the bottom oven; the pie looked very comfortable.

Ribby put on her shawl and bonnet and went out again with a basket to the village shop to buy a packet of tea, a pound of lump sugar and a pot of marmalade.

And just at the same time, Duchess came out of *her* house at the other end of the village.

Ribby met Duchess halfway down the street, also carrying a basket, but hers was covered with a cloth. They only bowed to one another; they did not speak, because they were going to have a party.

The Pie and the Patty-Pan

Ribby went to the farm, to fetch milk and butter

As soon as Duchess had got round the corner out of sight – she simply ran! Straight away to Ribby's house!

Ribby went into the shop and bought what she required and came out after a pleasant gossip with cousin Tabitha Twitchit.

Cousin Tabitha was disdainful afterwards in conversation: 'A little *dog* indeed!

The Pie and the Patty-Pan

Duchess with the veal-and-ham pie

Just as if there were no *cats* in Sawrey!
And a *pie* for afternoon tea! The very
idea!' said Cousin Tabitha Twitchit.

Ribby went on to Timothy Baker's
and bought the muffins. Then she went
home.

There seemed to be a sort of scuffling
noise in the back passage as she was
coming in at the front-door.

'I trust that is not that magpie: the spoons are locked up, however,' said Ribby.

But there was nobody there.

Ribby opened the bottom oven door, with some difficulty, and turned the pie. There began to be a pleasing smell of baked mouse!

Duchess, in the meantime, had slipped out at the back door.

'It is a very odd thing that Ribby's pie was *not* in the oven when I put mine in! And I couldn't find it anywhere; I looked all over the house. I put *my* pie into a nice hot oven at the top. I could not turn any of the other handles; I think that they are all shams,' said Duchess, 'but I wish I could have removed the pie made of

Duchess searches for the pie made of mouse

mouse! I cannot think what she has done with it. I heard Ribby coming and I had to run out by the back door!'

Duchess went home and brushed her beautiful black coat; and then she picked a bunch of flowers in her garden as a present for Ribby; and passed the time until the clock struck four.

Ribby — having assured herself by careful search that there was really no one hiding in the cupboard or in the larder — went upstairs to change her dress.

She put on a lilac silk gown, for the party, and an embroidered muslin apron and tippet.

'It is very strange,' said Ribby, 'I did not *think* I left that drawer pulled out; has somebody been trying on my mittens?'

She came downstairs again, and made the tea, and put the teapot on the hob. She peeped again into the *bottom* oven: the pie had become a lovely brown, and it was steaming hot.

She sat down before the fire to wait for the little dog. 'I am glad I used the *bottom* oven,' said Ribby, 'the top one

would certainly have been very much too hot. I wonder why that cupboard door was open? Can there really have been someone in the house?'

Very punctually, at four o'clock, Duchess started to go to the party. She ran so fast through the village that she was too early, and she had to wait a little while in the lane that leads down to Ribby's house.

'I wonder if Ribby has taken *my* pie

out of the oven yet?' said Duchess; 'but whatever can have become of the other pie made of mouse?'

At a quarter past four to the minute, there came a most genteel little tap-tappity. 'Is Mrs Ribston at home?' enquired Duchess in the porch.

'Come in! and how do you do, my dear Duchess?' cried Ribby. 'I hope I see you well?'

'Quite well, I thank you, and how do *you* do, my dear Ribby?' said Duchess. 'I've brought you some flowers; what a delicious smell of pie!'

'Oh, what lovely flowers! Yes, it is mouse and bacon!'

'It sounds delicious, my dear Ribby,' said Duchess; 'what a lovely white

Duchess in the porch

tablecloth! . . . Is it done to a turn? Is it still in the oven?'

'I think it wants another five minutes,' said Ribby. 'Just a shade longer; I will pour out the tea, while we wait. Do you take sugar, my dear Duchess?'

'Oh yes, please! my dear Ribby; and may I have a lump upon my nose?'

'With pleasure, my dear Duchess; how beautifully you beg! Oh, how sweetly pretty!'

Duchess sat up with the sugar on her nose and sniffed – 'How good that pie smells! I do love veal and ham – I mean to say mouse and bacon – '

She dropped the sugar in confusion, and had to go hunting under the tea-

table, so did not see which oven Ribby opened in order to get out the pie.

Ribby set the pie upon the table; there was a very savoury smell.

Duchess came out from under the tablecloth munching sugar, and sat up on a chair.

'I will first cut the pie for you; I am going to have muffin and marmalade,' said Ribby.

'Do you really prefer muffin? Mind the patty-pan!'

'I beg your pardon?' said Ribby.

'May I pass you the marmalade?' said Duchess hurriedly.

The pie proved extremely toothsome, and the muffins light and hot. They disappeared rapidly, especially the pie!

'I think' – thought the Duchess to herself – 'I *think* it would be wiser if I helped myself to pie; though Ribby did not seem to notice anything when she was cutting it. What very small fine pieces it has cooked into! I did not remember that I had minced it up so fine; I suppose this is a quicker oven than my own.'

'How fast Duchess is eating!' thought Ribby to herself, as she buttered her fifth muffin.

The pie-dish was emptying rapidly! Duchess had had four helps already and was fumbling with the spoon.

'A little more bacon, my dear Duchess?' said Ribby.

'Thank you, my dear Ribby; I was only feeling for the patty-pan.'

'The patty-pan, my dear Duchess?'

'The patty-pan that held up the pie-crust,' said Duchess, blushing under her black coat.

'Oh, I didn't put one in, my dear Duchess,' said Ribby. 'I don't think that it is necessary in pies made of mouse.'

Duchess fumbled with the spoon – 'I can't find it!' she said anxiously.

'There isn't a patty-pan,' said Ribby, looking perplexed.

'Yes, indeed, my dear Ribby; where can it have gone to?' said Duchess.

'There most certainly is not one, my dear Duchess. I disapprove of tin articles in puddings and pies. It is most undesirable – especially when people swallow in lumps!' she added in a lower voice.

The Pie and the Patty-Pan

'Thank you, my dear Ribby; I was only
feeling for the patty-pan.'

Duchess looked very much alarmed, and continued to scoop the inside of the pie-dish.

'My Great-Aunt Squintina — grand-mother of Cousin Tabitha Twitchit — died of a thimble in a Christmas plum-pudding. I never put any article of metal in *my* puddings or pies.'

Duchess looked aghast, and tilted up the pie-dish.

'I have only four patty-pans, and they are all in the cupboard.'

Duchess set up a howl. 'I shall die! I shall die! I have swallowed a patty-pan! Oh, my dear Ribby, I do feel so ill!'

'It is impossible, my dear Duchess; there was not a patty-pan.'

Duchess moaned and whined and rocked herself about. 'Oh, I feel so dreadful. I have swallowed a patty-pan!'

'There was *nothing* in the pie,' said Ribby severely.

'Yes there *was*, my dear Ribby, I am sure I have swallowed it!'

'Let me prop you up with a pillow, my dear Duchess; where do you think you feel it?'

'Oh, I do feel so ill *all over* me, my dear

Ribby; I have swallowed a large tin patty-pan with a sharp scalloped edge!'

'Shall I run for the doctor? I will just lock up the spoons!'

'Oh yes, yes! fetch that magpie Dr Maggotty, my dear Ribby: being a pie himself, he will certainly understand.'

Ribby settled Duchess in an armchair before the fire, and went out and hurried to the village to look for the doctor.

She found him at the smithy.

He was occupied in putting rusty nails into a bottle of ink, which he had obtained at the post office.

'Gammon? Ha! *Ha!*' said he, with his head on one side.

Ribby explained that her guest had swallowed a patty-pan.

The Pie and the Patty-Pan

*Dr Maggotty was putting rusty nails into
a bottle of ink*

'Spinach? Ha! *Ha!*' said he, and accompanied her with alacrity.

He hopped so fast that Ribby had to run. It was most conspicuous. All the village could see that Ribby was fetching the doctor.

'I *knew* they would over-eat themselves!' said Cousin Tabitha Twitchit.

But while Ribby
had been hunting
for the doctor –
a curious thing
had happened
to Duchess, who
had been left by
herself, sitting before the fire, sighing
and groaning and feeling very unhappy.

'How *could* I have swallowed it? Such
a large thing as a patty-pan!'

She got up and went to the table, and
felt inside the pie-dish again with a
spoon.

'No; there is no patty-pan, and I put
one in; and nobody has eaten pie except
me, so I must have swallowed it!'

She sat down again, and stared

mournfully at the grate. The fire crackled and danced, and something sizz-z-zled!

Duchess started! She opened the door of the *top* oven; out came a rich steamy flavour of veal and ham, and there stood a fine brown pie — and through a hole in the top of the pie-crust there was a glimpse of a little tin patty-pan!

Duchess drew a long breath — 'Then I must have been eating *mouse*! . . . No wonder I feel ill . . . But perhaps I should feel worse if I had really swallowed a patty-pan!' Duchess reflected. 'What a very awkward thing to have to explain to Ribby! I think I will put *my* pie in the back-yard and say nothing about it.

When I go home, I will run round and take it away.'
She put it outside the back-door, and
sat down again by the fire and shut her eyes; when Ribby arrived with the doctor, she seemed fast asleep.

'Gammon. Ha! *Ha!*' said the doctor.

'I am feeling very much better,' said Duchess, waking up with a jump.

'I am truly glad to hear it! He has brought you a pill, my dear Duchess!'

'I think I should feel *quite* well if he only felt my pulse,' said Duchess,

backing away from the magpie, who sidled up with something in his beak.

'It is only a bread pill, you had much better take it; drink a little milk, my dear Duchess!'

'Gammon? Gammon?' said the doctor, while Duchess coughed and choked.

'Don't say that again!' said Ribby, losing her temper. 'Here, take this bread and jam, and get out into the yard!'

'Gammon and Spinach! Ha! Ha! *Ha!*' shouted Dr Maggotty triumphantly outside the back door.

'I am feeling very much better, my dear Ribby,' said Duchess. 'Do you not think that I had better go home before it gets dark?'

'Perhaps it might be wise, my dear Duchess. I will lend you a nice warm shawl, and you shall take my arm.'

'I would not trouble you for worlds; I feel wonderfully better. One pill of Dr Maggotty – '

'Indeed, it is most admirable, if it has cured you of a patty-pan! I will call directly after breakfast to ask how you have slept.'

Ribby and Duchess said goodbye affectionately, and Duchess started home. Halfway up the lane she stopped and looked back; Ribby had gone in and shut her door. Duchess slipped through the fence and ran round to the back of Ribby's house and peeped into the yard.

Upon the roof of the pigsty sat Dr Maggotty and three jackdaws. The jackdaws were eating pie-crust, and the magpie was drinking gravy out of a patty-pan.

'Gammon! Ha! *Ha!*' he shouted when he saw Duchess's little black nose peeping round the corner.

Duchess ran home feeling uncommonly silly!

When Ribby came out for a pailful of water to wash up the tea-things, she found a pink-and-white pie-dish lying smashed in the middle of the yard. The

patty-pan was under the pump, where Dr
Maggotty had considerately left it.

Ribby stared with amazement.

'Did you ever see the like! So there really was a patty-pan? . . . But *my* patty-pans are all in the kitchen cupboard. Well, I never did! . . . Next time I want to give a party, I will invite Cousin Tabitha Twitchit!'

The Tale of
Jeremy Fisher

For Stephanie from Cousin B

Once upon a time there was a frog called Mr Jeremy Fisher; he lived in a little damp house among the buttercups at the edge of a pond.

The water was all slippy-sloppy in the larder and in the back passage. But Mr Jeremy liked getting his feet wet; nobody ever scolded him, and he never caught a cold!

He was quite pleased when he looked
out and saw large drops of rain, splashing
in the pond —

'I will get some worms and go fishing and catch a dish of minnows for my dinner,' said Mr Jeremy Fisher. 'If I catch more than five fish, I will invite my friends Mr Alderman Ptolemy Tortoise and Sir Isaac Newton. The Alderman, however, eats salad.'

Mr Jeremy put on a mackintosh, and a pair of shiny galoshes; he took his rod and basket, and set off with enormous hops to the place where he kept his boat.

The boat was round and green and very like the other lily-leaves. It was tied to a water-plant in the middle of the pond.

The Tale of Jeremy Fisher

Mr Jeremy took a reed pole and pushed the boat out into open water. 'I know a good place for minnows,' said Mr Jeremy Fisher.

Mr Jeremy stuck his pole into the mud and fastened the boat to it. Then he settled himself cross-legged and arranged his fishing tackle. He had the dearest little red float. His rod was a tough stalk of grass, his line was a fine long white

horsehair, and he tied a little wriggling worm at the end.

The rain trickled down his back, and for nearly an hour he stared at the float.

'This is getting tiresome, I think I should like some lunch,' said Mr Jeremy Fisher.

He punted back again among the water-plants, and took some lunch out of his basket. 'I will eat a butterfly sandwich, and wait till the shower is over,' said Mr Jeremy Fisher.

A great big water-beetle came up underneath the lily leaf and tweaked the toe of one of his galoshes.

Mr Jeremy crossed his legs up shorter, out of reach, and went on eating his sandwich.

Once or twice something moved about with a rustle and a splash among the rushes at the side of the pond.

'I trust that is not a rat,' said Mr Jeremy Fisher; 'I think I had better get away from here.'

Mr Jeremy shoved the boat out again a little way, and dropped in the bait. There was a bite almost directly; the float gave a tremendous bobbit!

'A minnow! a minnow! I have him by the nose!' cried Mr Jeremy Fisher, jerking up his rod.

But what a horrible surprise! Instead of a smooth fat minnow, Mr Jeremy landed little Jack Sharp, the stickleback, covered with spines!

The Tale of Jeremy Fisher

The stickleback floundered about the boat, pricking and snapping until he was quite out of breath. Then he jumped back into the water.

And a shoal of other little fishes put their heads out, and laughed at Mr Jeremy Fisher. And while Mr Jeremy sat disconsolately on the edge of his boat —

sucking his sore fingers and peering down into the water — a *much* worse thing happened; a really *frightful* thing it would have been, if Mr Jeremy had not been wearing a mackintosh!

A great big enormous trout came up —

ker-pflop-p-p-p! with a splash – and it seized Mr Jeremy with a snap, 'Ow! Ow! Ow!' – and then it turned and dived down to the bottom of the pond!

But the trout was so displeased with the taste of the mackintosh that in less than half a minute it spat him out again; and the only thing it swallowed was Mr Jeremy's galoshes.

Mr Jeremy bounced up to the surface of the water, like a cork and the bubbles out of a soda-water bottle; and he swam with all his might to the edge of the pond.

He scrambled out on the first bank he came to, and he hopped home across the meadow with his mackintosh all in tatters.

'What a mercy that was not a pike!' said Mr Jeremy Fisher. 'I have lost my rod and basket; but it does not much matter, for I am sure I should never have dared to go fishing again!'

He put some sticking plaster on his fingers, and his friends both came to dinner. He could not offer them fish, but he had something else in his larder.

Sir Isaac Newton wore his black and gold waistcoat.

And Mr Alderman Ptolemy Tortoise
brought a salad with him in a string bag.

And instead of a nice dish of minnows, they had a roasted grasshopper with ladybird sauce, which frogs consider a beautiful treat; but *I* think it must have been nasty!

The Story of a
Fierce Bad Rabbit

This is a fierce bad rabbit; look at his savage whiskers and his claws and his turned-up tail.

Beatrix Potter

This is a nice gentle rabbit. His mother has given him a carrot.

The Story of a Fierce Bad Rabbit

The bad rabbit would like
some carrot.

He doesn't say, 'Please.' He takes it!

The Story of a Fierce Bad Rabbit

And he scratches the good
rabbit very badly.

Beatrix Potter

The good rabbit creeps away and
hides in a hole. It feels sad.

The Story of a Fierce Bad Rabbit

This is a man with a gun.

Beatrix Potter

He sees something sitting on a bench.
He thinks it is a very funny bird!

The Story of a Fierce Bad Rabbit

He comes creeping up behind
the trees.

And then he shoots – *bang!*

The Story of a Fierce Bad Rabbit

This is what happens —

Beatrix Potter

But this is all he finds on the bench
when he rushes up with his gun.

The Story of a Fierce Bad Rabbit

The good rabbit peeps out of
his hole . . .

Beatrix Potter

. . . and he sees the bad rabbit tearing
past – without any tail or whiskers!

The Story of Miss Moppet

This is a pussy called Miss Moppet; she thinks she has heard a mouse!

Beatrix Potter

This is the mouse peeping out from
behind the cupboard and making fun
of Miss Moppet. He is not afraid
of a kitten.

The Story of Miss Moppet

This is Miss Moppet jumping just too late; she misses the mouse and hits her own head.

Beatrix Potter

She thinks it is a very hard cupboard!

The Story of Miss Moppet

The mouse watches Miss Moppet from
the top of the cupboard.

Beatrix Potter

Miss Moppet ties up her head in a
duster and sits before the fire.

The Story of Miss Moppet

The mouse thinks she is looking
very ill. He comes sliding down
the bell pull.

Miss Moppet looks worse and worse.
The Mouse comes a little nearer.

The Story of Miss Moppet

Miss Moppet holds her poor head
in her paws and looks at him through
a hole in the duster. The mouse
comes *very* close.

And then all of a sudden –
Miss Moppet jumps upon
the mouse!

The Story of Miss Moppet

And because the mouse has teased
Miss Moppet, Miss Moppet
thinks she will tease the mouse,
which is not at all nice
of Miss Moppet.

She ties him up in the duster
and tosses it about like a ball.

The Story of Miss Moppet

But she forgot about that hole in
the duster; and when she untied
it – there was no mouse!

He has wriggled out and run away;
and he is dancing a jig on top
of the cupboard!

The Tale of
Tom Kitten

To all pickles — especially to those

that get up on my garden wall

Once upon a time there were three little kittens, and their names were Mittens, Tom Kitten and Moppet.

They had dear little fur coats of their own; and they tumbled about the doorstep and played in the dust.

But one day their mother – Mrs Tabitha Twitchit – expected friends to tea; so she fetched the kittens indoors, to wash and dress them, before the fine company arrived.

The Tale of Tom Kitten

First she scrubbed their faces (this one is Moppet).

Then she brushed their fur (this one is Mittens).

Then she combed their tails and whiskers (this is Tom Kitten).

Tom was very naughty, and he scratched.

Mrs Tabitha dressed Moppet and Mittens in clean pinafores and tuckers; and then she took all sorts of elegant uncomfortable clothes out of a chest of drawers in order to dress up her son Thomas.

The Tale of Tom Kitten

Tom Kitten was very fat, and he had grown; several buttons burst off. His mother sewed them on again.

When the three kittens were ready, Mrs Tabitha unwisely turned them out into the garden, to be out of the way while she made hot buttered toast.

'Now keep your frocks clean, children! You must walk on your hind legs. Keep away from the dirty ash-pit and from Sally Henny Penny and from the pigsty and the Puddle-Ducks.'

Moppet and Mittens walked down the garden path unsteadily. Presently they trod upon their pinafores and fell on their noses. When they stood up there were several green smears!

The Tale of Tom Kitten

'Let us climb up the rockery and sit on the garden wall,' said Moppet.

They turned their pinafores back to front and went up with a skip and a

jump; Moppet's white tucker fell down into the road.

Tom Kitten was quite unable to jump when walking upon his hind legs in trousers. He came up the rockery by degrees, breaking the ferns and shedding buttons right and left.

He was all in pieces when he reached the top of the wall. Moppet and Mittens tried to pull him together; his hat fell off and the rest of his buttons burst.

While they were in difficulties, there

was a pit pat, paddle pat! and the three
Puddle-Ducks came along the hard high
road, marching one behind the other and
doing the goose step – pit pat, paddle
pat! pit pat, waddle pat!

They stopped and stood in a row and stared up at the kittens. They had very small eyes and looked surprised.

Then the two duck-birds, Rebeccah and Jemima Puddle-Duck, picked up the hat and tucker and put them on.

Mittens laughed so that she fell off the wall. Moppet and Tom descended after her; the pinafores and all the rest of Tom's clothes came off on the way down.

'Come, Mr Drake Puddle-Duck!' said Moppet. 'Come and help us to dress him! Come and button up Tom!'

Mr Drake Puddle-Duck advanced in a slow sideways manner and picked up the various articles.

But he put them on *himself*! They fitted him even worse than Tom Kitten.

'It's a very fine morning!' said Mr Drake Puddle-Duck.

And he and Jemima and Rebeccah Puddle-Duck set off up the road, keeping step — pit pat, paddle pat! pit pat, waddle pat!

Then Tabitha Twitchit came down the garden and found her kittens on the wall with no clothes on.

She pulled them off the wall, smacked
them, and took them back to the house.

'My friends will arrive in a minute and you are not fit to be seen; I am affronted,' said Mrs Tabitha Twitchit.

She sent them upstairs; and I am sorry to say she told her friends that they were in bed with the measles – which was not true.

The Tale of Tom Kitten

Quite the contrary; they were not in bed: *not* in the least.

Somehow there were very extraordinary noises overhead, which disturbed the dignity and repose of the tea party.

The Tale of Tom Kitten

And I think that someday I shall have to make another, larger book, to tell you more about Tom Kitten!

As for the Puddle-Ducks – they went into a pond.

The clothes all came off directly, because there were no buttons.

And Mr Drake Puddle-Duck and Jemima and Rebeccah have been looking for them ever since.

The Tale of Jemima Puddle-Duck

A farmyard tale for Ralph and Betsy

What a funny sight it is to see a brood of ducklings with a hen! Listen to the story of Jemima Puddle-Duck, who was annoyed because the farmer's wife would not let her hatch her own eggs.

Her sister-in-law, Mrs Rebeccah Puddle-Duck, was perfectly willing to leave the hatching to someone else — 'I have not the patience to sit on a nest for twenty-eight days; and no more have you, Jemima. You would let them go cold; you know you would!'

The Tale of Jemima Puddle-Duck

'I wish to hatch my own eggs; I will hatch them all by myself,' quacked Jemima Puddle-Duck.

She tried to hide her eggs; but they were always found and carried off.

Jemima Puddle-Duck became quite desperate. She determined to make a nest right away from the farm.

She set off on a fine spring afternoon along the cart road that leads over the hill. She was wearing a shawl and a poke bonnet.

When she reached the top of the hill, she saw a wood in the distance. She thought that it looked a safe quiet spot.

Jemima Puddle-Duck was not much in the habit of flying. She ran downhill a few yards flapping her shawl and then she jumped off into the air.

She flew beautifully when she had got a good start. She skimmed along over the treetops until she saw an open place in the middle of the wood where the trees and brushwood had been cleared.

Jemima alighted rather heavily and began to waddle about in search of a convenient dry nesting place. She rather fancied a tree stump among some tall foxgloves.

But – seated upon the stump she was startled to find an elegantly dressed gentleman reading a newspaper. He had black prick ears and sandy-coloured whiskers.

'Quack?' said Jemima Puddle-Duck, with her head and her bonnet on one side – 'Quack?'

The gentleman raised his eyes above his newspaper and looked curiously at Jemima – 'Madam, have you lost your way?' said he.

He had a long bushy tail which he was

The Tale of Jemima Puddle-Duck

sitting upon, as the stump was somewhat
damp. Jemima thought him mighty civil
and handsome.

She explained that she had not lost her way but that she was trying to find a convenient dry nesting place.

'Ah! is that so? Indeed!' said the gentleman with sandy whiskers, looking curiously at Jemima. He folded up the newspaper and put it in his coat-tail pocket.

The Tale of Jemima Puddle-Duck

Jemima complained of the superfluous hen.

'Indeed! How interesting! I wish I could meet with that fowl. I would teach it to mind its own business!

'But as to a nest — there is no difficulty: I have a sackful of feathers in my wood-shed. No, my dear madam, you will be in nobody's way. You may sit there as long as you like,' said the bushy long-tailed gentleman.

He led the way to a very retired, dismal-looking house among the foxgloves. It was built of faggots and turf, and there were two broken pails, one on top of another, by way of a chimney.

'This is my summer residence; you would not find my earth — my winter

house – so convenient,' said the hospitable gentleman.

There was a tumbledown shed at the back of the house, made of old soap boxes. The gentleman opened the door and showed Jemima in. The shed was almost full of feathers – it was quite suffocating; but it was comfortable and very soft.

The Tale of Jemima Puddle-Duck

Jemima Puddle-Duck was rather surprised to find such a vast quantity of feathers. But it was very comfortable; and she made a nest without any trouble at all.

When she came out, the sandy-whiskered gentleman was sitting on a log reading the newspaper — at least he had

it spread out, but he was looking over the top of it. He was so polite that he seemed almost sorry to let Jemima go home for the night.

He promised to take great care of her nest until she came back again the next day. He said he loved eggs and ducklings;

he should be proud to see a fine nestful in his woodshed.

Jemima Puddle-Duck came every afternoon; she laid nine eggs in the nest. They were greeny white and very large. The foxy gentleman admired them immensely. He used to turn them over and count them when Jemima was not there.

At last Jemima told him that she intended to begin to sit next day — 'and I will bring a bag of corn with me, so that I need never leave my nest until the eggs are hatched. They might catch cold,' said the conscientious Jemima.

'Madam, I beg you not to trouble yourself with a bag; I will provide oats. But before you commence your tedious sitting, I intend to give you a treat. Let us have a dinner-party all to ourselves!

'May I ask you to bring up some herbs from the farm-garden to make a savoury omelette? Sage and thyme, and mint and two onions, and some parsley. I will provide lard for the stuff – lard for the

omelette,' said the hospitable gentleman with sandy whiskers.

Jemima Puddle-Duck was a simpleton: not even the mention of sage and onions made her suspicious.

She went round the farm-garden, nibbling off snippets of all the different

sorts of herbs that are used for stuffing roast duck.

And she waddled into the kitchen and got two onions out of a basket.

The collie-dog Kep met her coming out. 'What are you doing with those onions? Where do you go every afternoon by yourself, Jemima Puddle-Duck?'

Jemima was rather in awe of the collie; she told him the whole story.

The collie listened, with his wise head on one side; he grinned when she described the polite gentleman with sandy whiskers.

He asked several questions about the wood and about the exact position of the house and shed.

Then he went out, and trotted down the village. He went to look for two foxhound puppies who were boarded out with the butcher.

Jemima Puddle-Duck went up the cart road for the last time, on a sunny afternoon. She was rather burdened with bunches of herbs and two onions in a bag.

The Tale of Jemima Puddle-Duck

She flew over the wood, and alighted opposite the house of the bushy long-tailed gentleman.

He was sitting on a log; he sniffed the air and kept glancing uneasily round the wood.

When Jemima alighted he quite jumped.

'Come into the house as soon as you have looked at your eggs. Give me the herbs for the omelette. Be sharp!'

He was rather abrupt. Jemima Puddle-Duck had never heard him speak like that.

The Tale of Jemima Puddle-Duck

She felt surprised and uncomfortable. While she was inside she heard pattering feet round the back of the shed. Someone with a black nose sniffed at the bottom of the door and then locked it.

Jemima became much alarmed.

A moment afterwards there were most awful noises — barking, baying, growls and howls, squealing and groans.

And nothing more was ever seen of that foxy-whiskered gentleman.

Presently Kep opened the door of the shed and let out Jemima Puddle-Duck.

Unfortunately the puppies rushed in and gobbled up all the eggs before he could stop them.

He had a bite on his ear, and both the puppies were limping.

Jemima Puddle-Duck was escorted home in tears on account of those eggs.

She laid some more in June, and she was permitted to keep them herself: but

only four of them hatched. Jemima Puddle-Duck said that it was because of her nerves; but she had always been a bad sitter.

The Tale of
Pigling Bland

To Cecily and Charlie,
a tale of the Christmas pig

Once upon a time there was an old pig
called Aunt Pettitoes. She had a family
of eight: four little girl pigs, called Crosspatch, Suck-suck, Yock-yock and Spot;
and four little boy pigs, called Alexander,
Pigling Bland, Chin-chin and Stumpy.
Stumpy had had an accident to his tail.

The eight little pigs had very fine
appetites — 'Yus, yus, yus! they eat and
indeed they *do* eat!' said Aunt Pettitoes,

looking at her family with pride. Suddenly there were fearful squeals: Alexander had squeezed inside the hoops of the pig trough and stuck.

Aunt Pettitoes and I dragged him out by the hind legs.

Chin-chin was already in disgrace; it was washing day, and he had eaten a piece of soap. And presently, in a basket of clean clothes, we found another dirty little pig – 'Tchut, tut, tut! whichever is this?' grunted Aunt Pettitoes.

Now all the pig family are pink, or pink with black spots, but this pig child was smutty black all over; when it had been popped into a tub, it proved to be Yock-yock.

I went into the garden; there I found Crosspatch and Suck-suck rooting up carrots. I whipped them myself and led them out by the ears. Crosspatch tried to bite me.

'Aunt Pettitoes, Aunt Pettitoes! you are a worthy person, but your family is not well brought up. Every one of them has been in mischief except Spot and Pigling Bland.'

'Yus, yus!' sighed Aunt Pettitoes. 'And they drink bucketfuls of milk; I shall have to get another cow! Good little Spot shall stay at home to do the house-work; but the others must go. Four little boy pigs and four little girl pigs are too many altogether. Yus, yus, yus,' said

Aunt Pettitoes, 'there will be more to eat without them.'

So Chin-chin and Suck-suck went away in a wheelbarrow, and Stumpy,

Yock-yock and Crosspatch rode away in a cart.

And the other two little boy pigs, Pigling Bland and Alexander, went to market. We brushed their coats, we curled their tails and washed their little faces, and wished them goodbye in the yard.

Aunt Pettitoes wiped her eyes with a large pocket handkerchief, then she wiped Pigling Bland's nose and shed tears; then she wiped Alexander's nose and shed tears; then she passed the hand-kerchief to Spot.

Aunt Pettitoes sighed and grunted, and addressed those little pigs as follows: 'Now Pigling Bland, son Pigling Bland, you must go to market. Take your brother Alexander by the hand. Mind your Sunday clothes, and remember to blow your nose' — (Aunt Pettitoes passed round the handkerchief again) — 'beware of traps, hen roosts, bacon and eggs; always walk upon your hind legs.' Pigling Bland who was a sedate little pig, looked solemnly at his mother; a tear trickled down his cheek.

Aunt Pettitoes turned to the other —

'Now son Alexander take the hand' –
'Wee, wee, wee!' giggled Alexander –
'take the hand of your brother Pigling
Bland, for you must go to market.
Mind –'

'Wee, wee, wee!' interrupted Alexander again.

'You put me out,' said Aunt Pettitoes – 'Observe signposts and milestones; do not gobble herring bones – '

'And remember,' said I impressively, 'if you once cross the county boundary you cannot come back. Alexander, you are not attending. Here are two licences permitting two pigs to go to market in

Lancashire. Attend Alexander. I have had no end of trouble in getting these papers from the policeman.' Pigling Bland listened gravely; Alexander was hopelessly volatile.

I pinned the papers, for safety, inside their waistcoat pockets; Aunt Pettitoes gave to each a little bundle, and eight conversation peppermints with appropriate moral sentiments in screws of paper. Then they started.

Pigling Bland and Alexander trotted along steadily for a mile; at least Pigling Bland did. Alexander made the road half as long again by skipping from side to side. He danced about and pinched his brother, singing —

'This pig went to market, this pig stayed at home,
This pig had a bit of meat —

let's see what they have given *us* for dinner, Pigling.'

Pigling Bland and Alexander sat down and untied their bundles. Alexander gobbled up his dinner in no time; he had already eaten all his own peppermints — 'Give me one of yours, please, Pigling?'

'But I wish to preserve them for

emergencies,' said Pigling Bland doubt-
fully.

Alexander went into squeals of laughter.
Then he pricked Pigling with the pin

that had fastened his pig paper; and when Pigling slapped him he dropped the pin, and tried to take Pigling's pin, and the papers got mixed up. Pigling Bland reproved Alexander.

But presently they made it up again, and trotted away together, singing —

> *'Tom, Tom the piper's son, stole a pig and*
> *away he ran!*
> *But all the tune that he could play was*
> *"Over the hills and far away"!'*

'What's that, young sirs? Stole a pig? Where are your licences?' said the policeman. They had nearly run against him round a corner. Pigling Bland pulled out his paper; Alexander, after fumbling, handed over something scrumply —

' "To two and half ounces of conversation sweeties at three farthings" – What's this? this ain't a licence.'

Alexander's nose lengthened visibly; he had lost it. 'I had one, indeed I had, Mr Policeman!'

'It's not likely they let you start without. I am passing the farm. You may walk with me.'

'Can I come back too?' enquired Pigling Bland.

'I see no reason, young sir; your paper is all right.'

Pigling Bland did not like going on alone, and it was beginning to rain. But it is unwise to argue with the police; he gave his brother a peppermint, and watched him out of sight.

To conclude the adventures of

Alexander – the policeman sauntered up to the house about teatime, followed by a damp subdued little pig. I disposed of Alexander in the neighbourhood; he did fairly well when he had settled down.

Pigling Bland went on alone dejectedly; he came to a crossroads and a signpost – 'To Market Town, 5 miles', 'Over the Hills, 4 miles', 'To Pettitoes Farm, 3 miles'.

The Tale of Pigling Bland

Pigling Bland was shocked: there was little hope of sleeping in Market Town, and tomorrow was the hiring fair; it was deplorable to think how much time had been wasted by the frivolity of Alexander.

He glanced wistfully along the road towards the hills, and then set off walking obediently the other way, buttoning up his coat against the rain. He had never wanted to go; and the idea of standing all by himself in a crowded market, to be stared at and pushed, and hired by some big strange farmer, was very disagreeable:

'I wish I could have a little garden and grow potatoes,' said Pigling Bland.

He put his cold hand in his pocket and felt his paper, he put his other hand in his other pocket and felt another paper – Alexander's! Pigling squealed; then ran back frantically, hoping to overtake Alexander and the policeman.

He took a wrong turn — several wrong turns — and was quite lost.

It grew dark, the wind whistled, the trees creaked and groaned.

Pigling Bland became frightened and cried, 'Wee, wee, wee! I can't find my way home!'

After an hour's wandering he got out of the wood; the moon shone through the clouds, and Pigling Bland saw a country that was new to him.

The road crossed a moor; below was a wide valley with a river twinkling in the moonlight, and beyond – in the misty distance – lay the hills.

He saw a small wooden hut, made his way to it and crept inside – 'I am afraid it *is* a hen-house, but what can I do?' said Pigling Bland, wet and cold and quite tired out.

'Bacon and eggs, bacon and eggs!' clucked a hen on a perch.

'Trap, trap, trap! Cackle, cackle, cackle!' scolded the disturbed cockerel. 'To market, to market! Jiggetty-jig!' clucked a broody white hen roosting next to him. Pigling Bland, much alarmed, determined to leave at daybreak. In the meantime, he and the hens fell asleep.

In less than an hour they were all awakened. The owner, Mr Peter Thomas

Piperson, came with a lantern and a hamper to catch six fowls to take to market in the morning.

He grabbed the white hen roosting next to the cock; then his eye fell upon

Pigling Bland, squeezed up in a corner. He made a singular remark — 'Hallo, here's another!' — seized Pigling by the scruff of the neck, and dropped him into the hamper. Then he dropped in five more dirty, kicking, cackling hens upon the top of Pigling Bland.

The hamper containing six fowls and a young pig was no light weight; it was taken downhill, unsteadily, with jerks. Pigling, although nearly scratched to pieces, contrived to hide the papers and peppermints inside his clothes.

At last the hamper was bumped down upon a kitchen floor, the lid was opened and Pigling was lifted out. He looked up, blinking, and saw an offensively ugly elderly man, grinning from ear to ear.

'This one's come of himself, whatever,' said Mr Piperson, turning Pigling's pockets inside out. He pushed the hamper into a corner, threw a sack over it to keep the hens quiet, put a pot on the fire and unlaced his boots.

Pigling Bland drew forward a coppy stool, and sat on the edge of it, shyly warming his hands. Mr Piperson pulled off a boot and threw it against the wainscot at the farther end of the kitchen. There was a smothered noise — 'Shut up!' said Mr Piperson. Pigling Bland warmed his hands, and eyed him.

Mr Piperson pulled off the other boot and flung it after the first, there was again a curious noise — 'Be quiet, will ye?' said Mr Piperson. Pigling Bland sat on the very edge of the coppy stool.

Mr Piperson fetched meal from a chest

and made porridge. It seemed to Pigling that something at the farther end of the kitchen was taking a suppressed interest in the cooking; but he was too hungry to be troubled by noises.

Mr Piperson poured out three platefuls: for himself, for Pigling and a third, which — after glaring at Pigling — he put away with much scuffling and locked up. Pigling Bland ate his supper discreetly.

After supper Mr Piperson consulted an almanac and felt Pigling's ribs; it was too late in the season for curing bacon and he grudged his meal. Besides, the hens had seen this pig.

He looked at the small remains of a flitch [side of bacon], and then looked undecidedly at Pigling. 'You may sleep on the rug,' said Mr Peter Thomas Piperson.

Pigling Bland slept like a top. In the morning Mr Piperson made more porridge; the weather was warmer. He looked to see how much meal was left in the chest and seemed dissatisfied — 'You'll likely be moving on again?' said he to Pigling Bland.

Before Pigling could reply, a neighbour, who was giving Mr Piperson and the hens a lift, whistled from the gate. Mr Piperson hurried out with the hamper, enjoining Pigling to shut the door behind him and not meddle with

nought; or 'I'll come back and skin ye!' said Mr Piperson.

It crossed Pigling's mind that if *he* had asked for a lift, too, he might still have been in time for market.

But he distrusted Peter Thomas.

After finishing breakfast at his leisure, Pigling had a look round the cottage; everything was locked up. He found some potato peelings in a bucket in the back kitchen. Pigling ate the peel, and washed up the porridge plates in the bucket. He sang while he worked –

> *'Tom with his pipe made such a noise,*
> *He called up all the girls and boys –*
> *And they all ran to hear him play,*
> *"Over the hills and far away"!'*

Suddenly a little smothered voice chimed in –

> *'Over the hills and a great way off,*
> *The wind shall blow my top-knot off!'*

Pigling Bland put down a plate which he was wiping, and listened.

After a long pause, Pigling went on tiptoe and peeped round the door into the front kitchen; there was nobody there.

After another pause, Pigling approached the door of the locked cupboard, and snuffed at the keyhole. It was quite quiet.

After another long pause, Pigling pushed a peppermint under the door. It was sucked in immediately.

In the course of the day Pigling pushed in all his remaining six peppermints.

When Mr Piperson returned, he found Pigling sitting before the fire; he had brushed up the hearth and put on the pot to boil; the meal was not get-at-able.

Mr Piperson was very affable; he

slapped Pigling on the back, made lots of porridge and forgot to lock the meal chest. He did lock the cupboard door; but without properly shutting it. He went to bed early, and told Pigling upon no account to disturb him next day before twelve o'clock.

Pigling Bland sat by the fire, eating his supper.

All at once at his elbow, a little voice

spoke – 'My name is Pig-wig. Make me more porridge, please!' Pigling Bland jumped, and looked round.

A perfectly lovely little black Berkshire pig stood smiling beside him. She had twinkly little screwed-up eyes, a double chin and a short turned-up nose.

She pointed at Pigling's plate; he

hastily gave it to her, and fled to the meal chest — 'How did you come here?' asked Pigling Bland.

'Stolen,' replied Pig-wig, with her mouth full.

Pigling helped himself to meal without scruple. 'What for?'

'Bacon, hams,' replied Pig-wig cheerfully.

'Why on earth don't you run away?' exclaimed the horrified Pigling.

'I shall after supper,' said Pig-wig decidedly.

Pigling Bland made more porridge and watched her shyly.

She finished a second plate, got up, and looked about her, as though she were going to start.

'You can't go in the dark,' said Pigling Bland.

Pig-wig looked anxious.

'Do you know your way by daylight?'

'I know we can see this little white house from the hills across the river. Which way are *you* going, Mr Pig?'

'To market – I have two pig papers. I might take you to the bridge; if you have no objection,' said Pigling much confused and sitting on the edge of his coppy stool. Pig-wig's gratitude was so touching and she asked so many questions that it became embarrassing to Pigling Bland.

He was obliged to shut his eyes and pretend to sleep. She became quiet, and there was a smell of peppermint.

'I thought you had eaten them?' said Pigling, waking suddenly.

'Only the corners,' replied Pig-wig, studying the sentiments with much interest by the firelight.

'I wish you wouldn't; he might smell them through the ceiling,' said the alarmed Pigling.

Pig-wig put back the sticky pepper-mints into her pocket; 'Sing something,' she demanded.

'I am sorry . . . I have toothache,' said Pigling, much dismayed.

'Then I will sing,' replied Pig-wig, 'You will not mind if I say ti idditty? I have forgotten some of the words.'

Pigling Bland made no objection; he sat with his eyes half shut, and watched her.

She wagged her head and rocked about, clapping time and singing in a sweet little grunty voice —

'A funny old mother pig lived in a stye, and
three little piggies had she;
Ti idditty idditty umph, umph, umph!
and the little pigs said wee, wee!'

She sang successfully through three
or four verses, only at every verse her
head nodded a little lower, and her little
twinkly eyes closed up —

'Those three little piggies grew peaky and lean,
*   and lean they might very well be;*
For somehow they couldn't say umph, umph,
* umph! and they wouldn't say wee, wee, wee!*
For somehow they couldn't say —'

Pig-wig's head bobbed lower and lower, until she rolled over, a little round ball, fast asleep on the hearth-rug.

Pigling Bland, on tiptoe, covered her up with an antimacassar.

He was afraid to go to sleep himself; for the rest of the night he sat listening to the chirping of the crickets and to the snores of Mr Piperson overhead.

Early in the morning, between dark and daylight, Pigling tied up his little bundle and woke up Pig-wig. She was excited and half-frightened. 'But it's dark! How can we find our way?'

'The cock has crowed; we must start

before the hens come out; they might shout to Mr Piperson.'

Pig-wig sat down again, and commenced to cry.

'Come away, Pig-wig; we can see when we get used to it. Come! I can hear them clucking!'

Pigling had never said shuh! to a hen in his life, being peaceable; also he remembered the hamper.

He opened the house door quietly and shut it after them. There was no garden; the neighbourhood of Mr Piperson's was all scratched up by fowls. They slipped away, hand in hand, across an untidy field to the road.

The sun rose while they were crossing the moor, a dazzle of light over the tops

of the hills. The sunshine crept down the slopes into the peaceful green valleys, where little white cottages nestled in gardens and orchards.

'That's Westmorland,' said Pig-wig. She dropped Pigling's hand and commenced to dance, singing —

'Tom, Tom the piper's son, stole a pig and
away he ran!
But all the tune that he could play, was
"Over the hills and far away"!'

'Come, Pig-wig, we must get to the bridge before folks are stirring.'

'Why do you want to go to market, Pigling?' enquired Pig-wig presently.

'I don't; I want to grow potatoes.'

'Have a peppermint?' said Pig-wig.

Pigling Bland refused quite crossly.

'Does your poor toothy hurt?' enquired Pig-wig.

Pigling Bland grunted.

Pig-wig ate the peppermint herself, and followed the opposite side of the road.

'Pig-wig! keep under the wall, there's a man ploughing.'

Pig-wig crossed over and they hurried downhill towards the county boundary.

Suddenly Pigling stopped; he heard wheels.

Slowly jogging up the road below them came a tradesman's cart. The reins flapped on the horse's back, the grocer was reading a newspaper.

'Take that peppermint out of your mouth, Pig-wig, we may have to run. Don't say one word. Leave it to me.

And in sight of the bridge!' said poor Pigling, nearly crying. He began to walk frightfully lame, holding Pig-wig's arm.

The grocer, intent upon his newspaper, might have passed them if his horse had not shied and snorted. He pulled the cart crossways, and held down his whip. 'Hello? Where are *you* going to?'

Pigling Bland stared at him vacantly.

'Are you deaf? Are you going to market?' Pigling nodded slowly.

'I thought as much. It was yesterday. Show me your licence.'

Pigling stared at the off-hind shoe of the grocer's horse which had picked up a stone.

The grocer flicked his whip – 'Papers? Pig licence?' Pigling fumbled in all his pockets, and handed up the papers. The grocer read them, but still seemed dissatisfied. 'This here pig is a young

lady; is her name Alexander?' Pig-wig opened her mouth and shut it again; Pigling coughed asthmatically.

The grocer ran his finger down the advertisement column of his news-paper – 'Lost, stolen or strayed, ten shillings reward'; he looked suspiciously at Pig-wig. Then he stood up in the trap, and whistled for the ploughman.

'You wait here while I drive on and speak to him,' said the grocer, gathering up the reins. He knew that pigs could be slippery; but surely, such a *very* lame pig could never run!

'Not yet, Pig-wig, he will look back.' The grocer did so; he saw the two pigs stock-still in the middle of the road. Then he looked over at his horse's heels; it was lame also; the stone took some

time to knock out after he got to the
ploughman.

'Now, Pig-wig, *now!*' said Pigling
Bland.

Never did any pigs run as these pigs

ran! They raced and squealed and pelted down the long white hill towards the bridge. Little fat Pig-wig's petticoats fluttered, and her feet went pitter, patter, pitter, as she bounded and jumped.

They ran, and they ran, and they ran down the hill, and across a short cut on level green turf at the bottom, between pebble beds and rushes.

They came to the river, they came to

the bridge – they crossed it hand in hand – then over the hills and far away Pig-wig danced with Pigling Bland!

Appley Dapply's Nursery Rhymes

Beatrix Potter

Appley Dapply, a little brown mouse,
Goes to the cupboard in
somebody's house.

Appley Dapply's Nursery Rhymes

In somebody's cupboard
There's everything nice:
Cake, cheese, jam, biscuits,
— All charming for mice!

Appley Dapply has little sharp eyes,
And Appley Dapply is *so* fond of pies!

Appley Dapply's Nursery Rhymes

Now who is this knocking at
Cottontail's door?
Tap tappit! Tap tappit!
She's heard it before!

And when she peeps out there
is nobody there,
But a present of carrots
put down by the stair.

Appley Dapply's Nursery Rhymes

Hark! I hear it again!
Tap, tap, tappit! Tap, tappit!
Why – I really believe it's a
little black rabbit!

Beatrix Potter

Old Mr Pricklepin has never a
cushion to stick his pins in.
His nose is black and his beard is grey,
And he lives in an ash stump
over the way.

Appley Dapply's Nursery Rhymes

You know the old woman who
lived in a shoe?
And had so many children
She didn't know what to do?

Beatrix Potter

I think if she lived in a little
shoe-house –
That little old woman was
surely a mouse!

Diggory Diggory Delvet!
A little old man in black velvet;
He digs and he delves —
You can see for yourselves
The mounds dug by Diggory Delvet.

Beatrix Potter

Gravy and potatoes
In a good brown pot –
Put them in the oven,
And serve them very hot!

Appley Dapply's Nursery Rhymes

There once was an amiable guinea-pig,
Who brushed back his hair like a
periwig;

Beatrix Potter

He wore a sweet tie,
As blue as the sky,
And his whiskers and buttons
Were very big.